For Greg
Here's a book [illegible] our chil[illegible]
hope for children's
and their children's future!
Your dear friend
Kwami Nyamidie
4-11-2017

Thirst No More

CreateSpace Independent Publishing Platform

Thirst No More

A Fable of Hope and Forgiveness

Kwami Nyamidie

Illustrations by
Nicole Stremlow Monahan

CreateSpace Independent Publishing Platform

ISBN-13: 9781541289239

ISBN-10: 1541289234

Library of Congress Control Number: 2016921444

Dedicated to you, the reader.

Table Of Contents

Prologue

Feno the tortoise helped the inhabitants of Tutiland to weather a severe drought that almost wiped them out. For his leadership in crisis, Feno gained worldwide recognition, and communities all over the world paid a fortune to find out his secret. Here is Feno's story.

Chapter 1

"Fear-No-One!" he yelled. It was his habit to call Feno's full name when the little one was in trouble.

Negu waited for a response. The dim light of the summer dawn streamed through the entrance to the cave home to which he would soon say good-bye.

"Fear-No-One!" Negu stretched his scaly neck from his shell and shouted out a second time. His voice pierced through the quiet morning like an arrow shooting through plantain leaves.

"Fear-No-One, It's time to go." He called for the third time, but there was no answer.

"Where's your son?" The head of the tortoise family turned to his wife.

"I don't know."

"We told him we'd be leaving this morning."

"We did."

"I don't want to stay here one day longer."

Negu dragged himself back into the cave. Iage followed. Together, they searched the cave's hidden pathways. To the right of the dark underground home hid a tunnel where Feno had played as a child. They looked under the dry leaves, but they did not find him. They searched outside the cave, looking for him.

"Come and see," Iage called for her husband.

"Is he there?"

"No."

Iage pointed to houseflies that swarmed the carcass of an antelope rotting away with maggots on the parched grass.

"Here's the fate awaiting us if we do not leave," Negu said.

"What are we going to do now that we can't find Feno?" Iage asked.

"Leave him behind, of course."

"What?"

"He knows where we're headed."

"And?"

"He can find us."

"We can't leave him behind. We just lost our baby. Can you bear losing him, too?" Iage said. She crawled away from the stench of the decaying animal, her flat shell cold with dry morning air.

A few weeks earlier, they had lost their six-month-old baby, who had succumbed to the devastating drought.

With his dome-shaped shell, Negu crawled out of the cave, a huge stone grotto that had been their protection for generations.

It was the day the tortoise family had planned to leave Tutiland, the drought-stricken savannah homeland, for Avaland, the forest where they hoped to start a better life. The nearby anthills that had fed them with lush plants and giant mushrooms in Tutiland now stared at them, incapable, because rains had stopped falling, like a dear friend who has lost the abilities on which everyone depends. The harsh heat had baked dry the orange-clay hills. Husband and wife were set to go for greener pastures in Avaland. But their twenty-two-year-old son (equivalent to an eleven-year-old for human beings) was nowhere to be found.

"I'm sick and tired of this place." Tears trickled down from Negu's sharp eyes.

Chapter 2

Several hours later, Iage heard the scratchy noise of dry leaves behind the cave.

"Where have you been?" she asked as Feno crept out with his short and stocky legs.

"I went to say good-bye to my friends," Feno said.

"Which friends?" Iage asked.

"Esebu the blue butterfly. She lives with her family in the half-dead acacia tree."

"You? Friends with the blue butterfly?" Negu asked.

"When Esebu was a caterpillar creeping on the ground, I rescued her from ants that wanted to eat her," Feno said.

"Wonderful. But time to go. Look, the sun is high up. It's getting too late," Negu scolded him.

"I don't want to go."

"You were the one dreaming of a better place," Iage said.

Before the family decided to leave the drought-stricken Tutiland, Feno had a recurring dream in which insects flipped about in tall, luxuriant grass. Birds and animals frolicked in trees alive with swaying branches. In his sleep, he quenched his unbearable thirst in an overflowing river. He feasted on acres of mushrooms growing by the hillside and swam for long dream hours, feeling the cool water refreshing his dry and hardened shell.

Negu convinces Feno that his dreams of a land flowing with rivers, verdant plant and blooming flowers may come true in the new land they were migrating to.

When he woke up, he recounted his vivid nighttime adventures to his family. His parents dismissed them as fantasy, of course. Everywhere around them told the story of the devastating drought: Dry riverbeds with gray bones of dried fish, smelly shells of dead crabs, and remains of rotten tadpoles. Scorched hills and fields screamed under the dry, hot winds blowing dust, dry leaves, feathers, and debris of putrefying remains. From every side, death's sickening smell enveloped them. His dreams contradicted what they were experiencing.

Imagine his surprise when he heard his mother referring to his dreams.

"Yes, but—" Feno said.

"Didn't you see your sister die when Koli refused to give her water?" Negu asked.

Koli, Tutiland's elephant king, had taken over the only available source of water.

"But I'm scared," Feno said.

"I'm scared, too," Iage said.

"Why don't you want to leave this horrible place?" Negu rolled his long neck midway back into his concave shell. The rays of the morning sun streamed down from above the hills and bounced off his eyes.

"This is the only home I know. I'm afraid of losing my friend. It's difficult to make new ones in a new place," Feno said.

Negu heaved a deep sigh. With all that had happened, Negu was baffled that he still had to convince them, especially Feno, who had seemed eager to leave.

"Why didn't we persist when we pleaded with Koli for the water for Fate?" Feno asked.

Koli kept the remaining source of water for his friends and blocked access to it to everyone else.

"Son, we did our best," Iage said.

"We must confront Koli before we leave," Feno said.

"Why?" Iage asked.

"To tell him we don't belong here. We belong in the sea. He should have treated us better," Feno said.

"Do you know what you're talking about? This is Koli, the elephant. Think about it." Negu paused. "This moving mountain on four legs! With his trunk, he can smash us into pieces."

"We can't run away from the place we've called home because of a tyrant," Feno said. "Let's tell him what we think."

"I'm surprised at you," Negu said to Iage.

"Surprised?" Iage asked.

"Yes. That we lost Fate, and you can't see what can happen to all of us here. We could all die," Negu said.

"We must find a safer place to live," Iage said.

"Well, how sure are you that we'll be safe where we're now headed?" Feno asked. "Everywhere we go, we'll be facing challenges: making a new life, adapting to an unknown place, and starting fresh relationships."

"The difficulties appear insurmountable," Iage said.

"Why don't we try talking to neighbors? We might be able to change Koli's mind.

He wasn't always this way," Feno suggested.

"How are you going to get most of Tutilanders in one place to ask Koli to change his mind? Let's cross the narrow bridge to Avaland. We'll know what to do next when we get there," Negu whose name means "never give up" said.

Tutiland, where the tortoise family lived, had only one outlet to Avaland, which had not yet experienced the severe drought. A dangerous ravine separated Tutiland from the outside world. Several years ago, Koli built a wooden bridge over the ravine. It was one of the accomplishments that endeared him to Tutilanders when he became king.

"I can't decide whether I want to come with you or stay behind," Feno said.

"Son, we have so many years ahead of us. If we can get out of here, at least we won't die of thirst," Negu said and turned to Feno. "Remember the dreams you've been having lately?"

"What about them?" Feno asked.

"They could come true in real life," Negu said.

"But you laughed at me when I recounted them," Feno said.

"Some dreams do come true," Iage said.

"OK then. Let's go," Feno said. "We can always come back. I really hate to lose this cave."

Chapter 3

Feno, Negu, and Iage left their home that late morning. They headed toward the narrow pass separating Tutiland from Avaland. They owned nothing, so leaving was easy. They trekked through the dry swath of parched land, past shrubs without leaves, drought-resistant date palms that dotted the land, and the rare, centuries-old baobab trees. Hot, dry, sandy winds blew on them as they trudged across the desolate grassland. Here and there, they found dead birds and animals that had succumbed to the drought.

On their way, they met Edi the white crane.

"Hey, guys! Where are you going?" Edi perched on the dirt path and walked along, pushing her long neck forward and backward while taking measured steps on the ground.

"We're leaving this terrible place," Negu told her.

"Terrible?" Edi asked.

"Yes, we're sick and tired of the drought," Iage said.

"And we want freedom," Negu said.

"Oh yeah," Edi said. She flapped her wings and hopped along. "But I really like it here."

"You do?" Negu said.

"Yes. Why don't you stay? This is a great place to be."

"Well, we've already made up our minds."

"Good luck," Edi said and flew away.

"I wonder how someone would like a place like this." Negu shook his head.

"Edi and her family are Koli's friends," Iage said. "Didn't you see them playing at the lake?"

She was referring to the unforgettable day they attempted to get water from the only remaining lake, which Koli guarded.

"I saw them. I saw the dung beetles too," Feno said. "They live on Koli."

Chapter 4

The tortoise family plodded on for several days. From time to time, they heard the growling of wolves, cheetahs, and leopards. They heard woodpeckers boring holes in dead trees and hungry hatchlings crying. Before sunset, on the third day, they met Zagadu the dung beetle.

"What are you up to?" Zagadu asked under the cloudless evening sky.

"We're just taking a walk," Negu said.

"I see." Zagadu rolled his round ball of herbivore droppings along and, without further comment, went away, guided by the Milky Way to his destination.

The setting sun cast its weakened light on a tired Negu, Iage, and Feno. Although it was dangerous, Negu believed they could cross the narrow bridge without difficulties.

They were getting close to the bridge, and in a matter of hours, they would arrive at Avaland, where plants still thrived. Even if they couldn't find running water, there would at least be dew they could suck on from leaves in the morning. That would keep them alive.

Feno dashed faster ahead to wait at the bridge for his parents. He thought of the friends he was going to miss. At least he would still have his parents. As he edged closer, Feno saw Koli standing near the bridge. He didn't see what he was doing there. Surprised, Feno raced back to alert his parents.

"Guess what!" Feno said.

"What is it?" Iage asked.

"Koli is standing by the bridge!"

"What?" Negu said.

"Koli is standing by the bridge. It looks like he's dragging something with his trunk."

"Why didn't you look to see what he was doing? Go back!" Negu stopped and looked into Iage's eyes.

"I'm not going alone." Feno said.

Chapter 5

Negu, Iage, and Feno got closer to the bridge and saw what Koli was up to. The elephant twirled his trunk around the wooden bridge and dragged it, making cracking noises as he broke it into chunks, with pieces hurtling into the abyss, releasing a sad rolling noise.

Teary, Iage looked into Negu's clear eyes. What were they going to do? Negu stood motionless for a while. Then he wobbled forward and stood before towering Koli.

"Why are you doing this?" Negu raised his head to ask.

Negu, Iage, and Feno got closer to the bridge and saw what Koli was up to.

Because I can," Koli said, looking down at Negu. "Because some ungrateful grassland dwellers are planning to leave my kingdom."

"You built this bridge. You dug wells that ensured we all Tutilanders had water in earlier droughts. You saved those who needed help. We loved you dearly and made you king as a result. Now we fear for our lives," Negu said. His shell was quaking. "And you watched our daughter die of thirst when it was in your power to save her."

"The blood of our daughter is on your hands," Iage said.

"Blame and more blame," Koli said. "Your child was dead before you arrived at the lake. Now you must blame it all on me. What else do you blame me for?"

"You should know that we're in this together. Instead, you play favorites and create winners and losers," Negu said.

"I wish you could be in my place for a day!" Koli trumpeted.

"I wish *you* could be in *ours* for just an hour," Negu said and shook his head.

"We're on our way to Avaland, in search of a better life." Iage raised her head in the direction of the lush vegetation beyond the ravine.

"Well," Koli said and raised his two front legs and twisted his trunk in the air. "You can't leave now. It's never going to happen."

"I thought the grassland dwellers were free to move anywhere they wanted," Negu said.

"To live anywhere they choose," Iage said.

"From where did you get that stupid idea?"

"I thought the desire to be free was as natural as breathing," Feno added. "Tell me, Koli —who taught you how to breathe?"

"No one."

"Just as nobody taught you how to breathe, no one taught us to desire freedom. It's inborn in all of us. Some of us have given up on you because of your wickedness. No wonder the other elephants left you long ago," Feno said.

When Koli became king, he had the support of his clan of elephants. One day, they all left. Rumor had it that they left because Koli was mean and unkind even to the little elephants. The matriarch elephants herded the little ones, and

Koli's male rivals left with the women and children.

"Ha-ha." Koli laughed. "I have many trustworthy friends."

"You mean those you've bribed. Those who benefit from you, citizens such as Zagadu the dung beetle and Edi the white crane, who live on what you don't need?" Feno asked.

Feno's remarks were too much for Koli to take.

"Who are you to talk back at me?" With his trunk, Koli grabbed and dangled the little tortoise in the air. Then he flung him into the ravine.

It happened so fast that Negu and Iage didn't have time to react until Feno was already out of sight.

Iage gasped in horror.

Negu was speechless.

The giant beast plodded toward Iage and raised his right foot, which he held in the air over her, threatening to stamp her to death.

"Please don't kill my wife," Negu said, still standing in front of Koli.

"She's my subject. I can kill her if I want," Koli said.

"I know you're the king. Spare my wife," Negu said, in tears. "Yes, you can, but please don't kill her."

Koli moved his right forward foot and rested it on Iage's shell. Iage felt the soft cushion of Koli's toes pressing on her back.

She was running out of breath, afraid that she would soon be crushed to death.

"Please, don't do it," Negu pleaded in tears.

Koli lifted his right foot as slowly as he could and placed his left forward foot, softly, on Iage's back. Negu feared that would be the end for his wife. This time, although Koli kept his foot over Iage for less than a minute, to Negu it felt like an eternity.

What would happen if he lost her? Their only son had just been thrown into the ravine. Their daughter had died of thirst. Negu's heart almost ceased beating.

He doubted everything he had believed about freedom. Negu always had believed that freedom was the air that kept the flame of life burning. Now, he did not know if that was true.

"Come for me instead," Negu shouted as though waking suddenly from a nightmare. "Please don't harm her. Kill me instead," he said. He felt guilty, as if he had led his family into disaster, even if that outcome had not been his intention.

Koli threatened to break Iage's back with his feet two more times. The third time, Negu pushed Iage from under Koli's foot. He wanted to suffer in her place.

Koli kicked Negu, thrusting him on a dry patch of stony ground some distance away.

Koli turned to Iage, who had almost passed out.

"Now you go get your stinky old husband. Return to your cave. And don't mess with me."Koli disappeared into the grassland twilight.

After calling their son's name and crying for hours,
Iage was convinced her son was dead

Chapter 6

Negu felt the pain of being hurled against a stone. The weight of his dome-shaped shell pressed against his body like a thousand prickling thorns. For a while he lay motionless. With difficulty, he tried to shove his legs out of his shell.

Negu was struggling and kicking his limbs in and out of his shell. He couldn't roll over onto his belly.

"Negu, are you OK?" she shouted.

Negu could not hear her.

"Are you OK?" Iage moved closer. "Can you reach up on top of me?" she asked. Negu attempted to grab her shell, but he could not. Iage pushed Negu with her side. After several attempts, she succeeded in flipping him over.

"Are you OK?"

"Oh, yes!" Negu said, feeling so much alive in her presence. "I'm fine. I thought you were going to die. So wonderful to hear your voice," Negu said, playing down the pain he was suffering.

"Thank you. I was very scared. To see him slam you away almost drained the life out of me."

"You're my one and only love," Negu said. "How could I live without you? I wanted to die in your place."

"Oh, Negu, you're so sweet. I, too, would die for you."Iage whose name means "I will never leave you" said.

"I wonder what's happening to Feno," Negu said.

"I don't know. I hope he's OK." Iage said.

"Me too, but the ravine is so deep that no one ever goes there and comes out alive."

"What do we do now?"

"Let's start looking for Feno right away."

The couple huddled together. So much had happened to them in such a short time that they felt as if they had been caught in a whirlwind. As they crawled toward the ravine, they kept talking.

"If we ever find him, we'll do what he suggested."

"Which is?"

"Gather all Tutilanders—birds and animals in the grassland—and see what we can do as a group about Koli."

"Why bother?"

"Why? He killed our daughter. And now he has thrown our son into the ravine. And he almost killed us."

"He's more powerful than us."

"But we must never give up."

"If you say so."

"Let's call out and see if Feno can hear us."

Chapter 7

Negu and Iage dragged themselves to the edge of the ravine near the broken bridge. "Fe-nooo!"

The gorge echoed back Iage's trembling voice, "Fe-nooo!"

Negu and Iage took turns calling their son without getting back a response.

They walked to the edge of the ravine, in the direction Koli had thrown him. No sight of him. No sounds of his cry. No moaning for help—only the indescribable and terrifying silence that covered the dark abyss.

"What shall we do next?" Negu asked.

"I don't know. We can't both throw

ourselves into the ravine."

After calling their son's name and crying for hours, Iage was convinced her son was dead.

"Maybe he's still alive," Negu comforted her.

"You think so?"

"Yes, he may be alive."

"OK, if you think he may be alive, let's keep vigil here for him."

Negu and Iage stayed awake by the ravine. Far away behind them, lightning had struck the dry leaves ablaze, and a fire raged into the early morning hours.

They hoped their son would be safe and able to climb out of the depths to meet them. It was the night of the dark moon, the last night before the new moon. Guided by the Milky Way, Zagadu the dung beetle rolled his wares along and ran into the couple, who were mourning their son.

"Nice to see you again," Zagadu said. "I thought you were on a journey."

"We didn't tell you that," Negu replied.

"Well, take good care of yourself. Just know that the king has large ears." Zagadu left his ball of elephant poop and crawled closer to the couple.

"By the way, when you have another child, raise him to respect his elders." With that insult, Zagadu went back to the stinky ball twice his size.

"You idiot," Iage shouted. "Who are you to tell me how to raise my child?"

"A word to the wise is enough," Zagadu said and rolled his stuff away.

Chapter 8

Negu and Iage went back home, convinced their son had died in the ravine. But they wanted to make sure he hadn't perished in vain, so they planned to let other Tutilanders know what had happened. They spread the news about Koli destroying the bridge, threatening their lives, hurling their son into the ravine, and causing their daughter's death.

One hot and sunny afternoon, Negu and Iage went to Tsali the lion. They told him what had happened to them. Would he help them avenge their son's death?

"Koli denied my daughter water, and she died. He hurled Feno, my son, into the pit. Who knows what he'll do to all of the remaining Tutilanders who are not in his good books!" Negu said.

"And you aren't particularly fond of Koli, either," Iage said.

"No, I'm not, but I can't imagine how I can help."

"You can use your influence to call a meeting of Tutilanders who have a bone to pick with Koli," Negu suggested.

"And we, as a community, can plan what to do about the water problem," Iage added.

"Water scarcity is a huge problem for us here. Any ideas on finding enough for all will be appreciated," Tsali said. "My wife is having problems nursing our cubs. But I still can't see how I can help."

Negu convinced Tsali to convene Tutilanders for a meeting. They met under a huge old baobab tree that had survived the long drought. The tree served as a gathering place but was also the home of weaverbirds and night owls. Mice and rats lived in the long, narrow hole of its trunk.

The rhinoceros, the python, the tiger, the hyena, and other Tutilanders came to hear Tsali. Others who had been blocked from leaving the dry grassland for the evergreen forest came.

"I've invited you so we can do something about Koli, the mean elephant," Tsali started.

"Like what?" Roko the monkey said, interrupting.

"Ask Koli to allow us to have the freedom to go where we want and to open the lake for everyone to drink," Tsali said.

"Koli won't listen to us," Atini the giraffe said.

"You must be joking, right?" Alu the rat asked. He spat out the palm nuts he had been hiding in his mouth. "Koli will simply squeeze some of us to death."

"You're right," said the small creatures of Tutiland in unison. "We can't fight Koli."

"Let me make an observation," Makutu the rabbit said. She flared her red nose and tweaked her silvery whiskers. "We can fight him. But we'll be beaten for sure."

"Yes, I understand your concerns. That's why I asked the tortoises to tell you their story, so we as a group can decide. What happened to this family can happen to any of us."

"Is there anyone here who hasn't heard what we have endured these past two months?" Negu asked.

Almost a month after Koli had scared the life out of Negu and Iage, some Tutilanders still had not heard their account, so Negu and his wife retold their story.

There were three groups at the gathering. Tsali's supporters found themselves in one party. They were ready to risk everything, even their lives, for a free and happy life. Then there were those who believed they were too small to win a fight against their mad and powerful ruler. This group teamed up with those who benefited in one way or the other from Koli.

"I disagree with how you are presenting Koli," Edi the white crane cut in. "You know that vegetation in Tutiland is turning dryer every season. Koli drinks a large amount of water. To survive, he must make sure there's enough for him and his friends. I take issue with you calling him a heartless tyrant."

"We know the only way you are making it here is by feeding on insects that bother Koli. You're his friend. But can't you see that by destroying the bridge, he made it difficult for all those who wanted to leave for other lands?"

Negu's outstretched neck lined with thick veins. He tried hard to hide the anger he felt when he heard Koli's defenders.

"Well, I'm not ashamed of Koli. I just wanted to make sure we have both sides of the story," Edi said and flew away.

The meeting continued, but within a short time, half of Tutilanders had gone.

From the distance, Tsali and his followers saw a dark moving image.

Roko the monkey climbed up the baobab tree. Many more of those gathered became afraid and ran away. Some attempted to cover themselves in the branches that had barely any leaves. Others hid in the hole inside its trunk. But Tsali and a few of the animals remained.

"Here comes Koli," Roko yelled.

Chapter 9

Koli stomped in.

"You can't mess with me," he said. "Edi the white crane was right in informing me that you are plotting against me."

"Yes, some of us want to go elsewhere," Tsali said.

"There's no food to eat," Iage said.

"No water to drink," Negu said.

"You have blocked access to the only source of water we have," Tsali said.

"We're suffering," Roko yelled from the tree.

"Our children are dying," Negu said.

"Don't mess with me," Koli growled

"We want you to do something about it," Tsali said.

"Ungrateful lot. I'm going to tear down this tree," Koli said. "That way you won't have any place to meet and plot against me."

"No, you won't tear down the tree," Tsali said.

"Yes, I will tear it down," Koli said.

"No, you won't."

"Yes, I will."

"No!"

"Yes!"

"No!"

Yes!"

Nakutu the eagle interrupted and pleaded with Koli, "Please don't pull down the tree. My baby eagles are there. And many other birds and animals live there. Look around. This is one of the few trees that have survived for as long as we can remember. It's our only shelter. Please don't destroy it."

"I don't care," Koli said. He raised his two front legs and twisted his trunk in the air. Koli took a deep breath and trumpeted. He twirled his strong trunk around the nearest branch and shook it. Nests fell from the branch. Broken birds' eggs scattered on dry leaves, littering the ground.

A monkey jumped out of the branches. Koli moved to wrap his trunk around the second branch. Tsali pounced and attempted to bite his trunk. Koli dodged Tsali. Tsali pounced back. For a few moments, everyone saw an angry Koli in action.

The red-brown clay ground on which they fought was turned up as if it had been plowed. Koli pushed Tsali back with his tusks. Tsali was relentless, charging and scratching Koli's thick skin.

Tsali pounced, attempting to claw Koli's face. Koli dodged Tsali, who landed on the hard surface away from the gathering. Koli followed him in the dust that gathered. He attempted to stick his tusks through Tsali's belly, but Tsali sprang away. Koli missed his target and stuck his tusks into the ground. Tsali attacked Koli from the back. Koli swerved and thrust his tusk into Tsali's side, grabbing the big cat by his throat, squeezing, and throwing him on the dusty ground.

Tsali lay soaked in his blood on the dry patch of land, gasping for breath.

"Don't mess with *me*," Koli growled. The monster king lifted his front legs and trunk. He broke off the remaining baobab branches and flung them away. More nests with eggs and little birds were scattered on the dry grass. Leaves and feathers fluttered in the dusty air. Bats flew out of the tree, shrieking in high-pitched surprise. Owls howled. Snakes slithered out of the holes hiding them.

Koli wasn't done yet. He twisted his trunk around the bare tree, attempting to pull it down. He shook the centuries-old baobab tree, but it was so huge that Koli's trunk couldn't encircle it. For once, Koli felt the frustration of coming up against his limits. Angered by his confrontation with this reality, Koli mustered all the power he had and clipped off the remaining branches.

"You can't mess with me." Koli turned to

leave after this incredible show of force. In his way lay a featherless eaglet with large scared eyes on her bald head. Shivering with fear, the eaglet cried for her mother.

Chapter 10

As Koli raised his heavy right foot to step on the helpless hatchling, Nakutu, a mother eagle, descended at the speed of light and swept her baby away. She carried the little one under her strong protective wings.

"Don't mess with me," the elephant said, looking with disbelief at Nakutu's swift rescue.

Confusion, despair, and helplessness seized the onlookers.

"What shall we do with Tsali, the wounded lion?" Negu asked.

Makutu touched Tsali, wondering if he was alive. Tsali was almost out of breath.

"Who would have guessed Koli had the

guts to tear down the baobab tree?" Nakutu asked.

"*You* brought this on to us,"Susu the bat said to Negu.

"Yes," said Tinya the mouse. "We have no water, and now we have no place to sleep."

"I feel powerless," said Dodo the armadillo. "How can we get out of this?"

"I feel so guilty," Negu said to Iage as they crawled back to their cave. "Maybe we should have kept quiet and mourned our son and daughter alone. Look at the pain and destruction crazy Koli has unleashed on all of us."

"I don't feel guilty. How do you think Fate and Fear-No-One would take it if they knew we forgot them? Weren't we doing what we felt was right to avenge their deaths?"

"Now I fear we've lost our friend Tsali the lion. We overestimated his strength. He was no match for Koli. And we all deserted him when he lay there helpless."

"We were all scared out of our minds. No doubt about that."

Husband and wife went home to their cave, feeling helpless. The new moon was setting. They had done all they possibly could. Negu felt powerless. Then a sense of worthlessness gripped him. It was more than four weeks after the terrible events that had led to their son's death.

"Since we can't beat Koli, maybe we should join his camp," Iage said.

"Are you out of your mind?"

"Things will be easier for us."

"What a terrible idea." Negu could not believe his wife's suggestion.

"We have no choice."

"This is very hard."

Just then, Negu and Iage heard a noise at the cave's dark entrance.

"Who's there?" Negu asked.

Chapter 11

When Koli threw Fear-No-One into the ravine, he expected the troublemaker to never see daylight again. But Feno landed on the steep edge of the ravine without falling into the abyss. He remained there in shock and unconscious for several days.

When he regained consciousness, he remembered vaguely the argument with Koli. He recollected saying something that had angered the elephant, who then wrapped his trunk—soft, muddy, and wrinkled—around him. Then all became a blur. He must have been thrown into the pit, he thought.

The young tortoise noticed a crack on his hard shell. How would he get out of this pit? How would his shell heal? What had happened to his parents? Were they alive?

As he became aware of his condition, Feno began to think about his life. How impossible for his recurrent dreams of a land green with life and overflowing with rivers to become real now that he found himself in the depth of darkness.

After another week in and out of wakefulness, he moved himself toward a stream of sunlight he saw beaming like a searchlight into the otherwise dark ravine. A few times, the rock he crawled over slid down the slope and rolled farther into the bottomless chasm. Several times, he narrowly missed tumbling into the abyss because he got stuck in a narrow gutter along the slope. In his final struggle upward, he climbed up to a flat land patch with plants growing along a spring. Sweet-smelling white lilies and other unusual flowers bloomed near the water. Ferns and creeping plants with orange leaves grew by the spring. Feno had not seen running water for years.

The water he drank from the spring refreshed and strengthened him.

Because scary rumors were told about how dangerous the ravine was, few Tutilanders dared to explore what was really there. Only a few insects, hummingbirds, and butterflies dared come to the spring.

"Blue butterfly, is that you?" Feno asked.

"Yes, I'm surprised to see you here," Esebu the blue butterfly said.

"You kept this place a secret from me? I thought you were my friend," Feno said.

"When did you learn to fly?" Esebu asked.

"Because I can't get to something I need, I shouldn't know about it?" Feno asked.

"I didn't want you to feel bad," Esebu said.

"What's the imagination for?" Feno asked.

"To envision what's possible," Esebu said. "Can you ever know what's possible?"

"Look right at me." Feno stood up with outstretched forelimbs. "What about that, my friend?"

Feno wanted to show Esebu the blue

butterfly that although it seemed impossible for him to ever come to the stream, somehow he found himself there.

"All right, all right, next time," Esebu said.

"Please don't keep this kind of secret from me in the future. Even if you thought I couldn't ever get here if you told me, it would still be nice to know there was a place like this."

"OK. Count on me. We'll always be friends."

Chapter 12

Feno discovered a whole new world of living things in a place that was supposed to have been his grave. For several days, he survived on unusual plants and mushrooms. Because he was still young, his broken carapace healed faster. Four weeks later, Feno climbed out of the ravine and headed home.

Even though he was doing better, he found himself limping. Getting over the hardship in the ravine energized him. If there was a safe place the family could go to, this was it. He would bring his parents to this secret place. Koli and his loyal friends would not reach them. He knew the lay of the ravine. He could show them where to step so they wouldn't fall into the abyss. But were his parents still alive?

As he struggled out of the ravine, Feno saw Edi the white crane. It felt like she was everywhere.

"You're still here?" Edi asked.

"Yes," Feno said and nodded.

"Koli said he threw you into the bottomless pit to teach you and your parents a lesson," Edi said.

"Surprise, surprise! I'm still kicking," Feno said. "To tell you the truth, I learned my lesson, but not what your tyrant master had in mind."

"Unbelievable. You learned a lesson?"

"Yes. Not to fear anyone. Our lives are in the hands of a superior power. That power controls everything. Even Koli."

"Can't argue with that if you survived being thrown into the abyss," Edi said and flew away.

Chapter 13

That night, with difficulty, Feno hobbled back home. As he came near the cave, his parents heard the dry leaves rustle. Alarmed, they called to find out who was there. Then, as if in a dream, the couple heard, "It's me."

Negu and Iage could not believe their ears.

"Feno," Iage called, "is that you?"

"Yes, I'm alive."

Negu and Iage kissed their son, touched him, and shed tears of joy.

"I never thought I would see you again," Iage said.

"I always knew you were alive. But it's

hard to believe what you can't see or touch," Negu said.

"I feel your broken shell," Iage said as she rubbed her motherly claws on her son's broken shell.

"Feno, can you tell us what happened to you?" Negu asked.

He told them about his experiences in the ravine, the seven days it took to recover his memory, his nearly falling into the bottomless pit, and realizing in the end how strong he truly was.

"I have a surprise for you," Feno said.

"A surprise?" Iage asked.

"While in the ravine, I discovered that the place isn't as fearful as we thought," Feno said.

"What do you mean?" Negu said.

"I discovered a water fountain with unusual plants and insects. But you have to know the way, and you must not be too big. Larger animals could slip into the pit."

"We can't make it there, can we?" Negu asked.

"We can make that place our hiding place. I

just came to get you."

"Oh, Feno, that's such good news." Iage smiled for the first time in days. "But I'm afraid. Over the years, we've heard about how dangerous the ravine is. I can't do it."

"Why, Mother? I thought you'd jump at such an opportunity."

"Well, so much has happened after we were separated four weeks ago," Negu said. "Today we did what you suggested. We got help from Tsali the lion, who invited many of the grassland dwellers, and we met at the old baobab tree to find ways to get Koli to see reason. We wanted to remind him how nice a ruler he used to be and how we would like him to return to his compassionate self. We also wanted to find ideas for solving the water problem."

"How did that turn out?"

"We barely started the meeting when Koli heard about it. He came and destroyed the branches of the baobab tree under which we were meeting. It was a total mess. Tsali fought him, but he was overpowered."

"Poor Tsali," Feno said.

"It was so sad," Iage said.

"I didn't know you would be that courageous—to pull off such a meeting," Feno said.

"We did, but we now regret what happened. The bats and owls and eagles have no home now. And Koli destroyed the nests, with all the nestlings and eggs in them."

"Very sad," Feno said.

"I thought we had no options left," Iage said.

"There must be a way to bring Koli to his knees. And it must not be through force," Feno said.

"How? I'm totally fed up and don't see how we can make our dream of being free come true," Negu said.

Feno hugged his mother.

"We're so glad you're alive," Iage said.

"So very happy," Negu said.

"I've come to show you a way out of this," Feno said.

"I still don't want to risk my life in the

ravine," Iage said.

"Why not?" Feno asked.

"Can't you see we are both bigger and heavier than you?" Negu asked.

"What we can do is limitless," Feno said.

"I can't promise that I will go down the ravine with you," Iage said. "Why don't we go and see the place you found before we decide?"

"In the morning, maybe?" Negu suggested. "I'm too tired now."

"Sure," Iage said.

"I believe there is a way to free ourselves from the elephant," Feno said.

"How?" Negu asked.

"Not sure. Certainly not by force," Feno said.

Chapter 14

Edi the white crane saw the juvenile tortoise coming out of the ravine and reported it to Koli.

"You have wings to go anywhere. Can you find out what the tortoise was doing?"

For the first time, Edi explored the ravine, and she reported back to Koli.

"The valley was dark and the slope steep. I wonder how the little tortoise survived without falling into the pit."

"If he could do it, some of the other small animals can do it too," Koli said.

"I doubt it," Edi said.

"The young tortoise and his parents will

likely go back." Koli paced and flapped his large ears. "We must stop them."

"How?"

"Bring me your family, all my friends, and my supporters."

"That's a disaster waiting to happen."

"Stop arguing with me."

"The ravine is truly dangerous."

"I said stop arguing with me!" Koli howled.

Against his will, Edi invited the beaver and all the little animals that resisted the plan to remove Koli as king.

"I've called you to thank you for standing by me in the lion's plot against me. Edi will take you to a secret water spring. That's my reward for your faithfulness. It's along a dangerous slope some of you can't reach, though."

"You want us to risk our lives?" the beaver asked.

"How can you say that?" Koli asked.

"Edi says the place is dangerous."

"How come the troublesome tortoise youngster survived it?" Koli wagged his tail. "Be careful."

Chapter 15

The following morning, after basking in the early-morning sunshine, Feno took his parents along to show them the new hiding place. Negu and Feno walked faster while Iage plodded behind.

"Where are you?" Negu asked.

Iage motioned them to go ahead. "I'm a little tired."

"We'll wait for you under the date palm over there," Negu said.

As they got to the date palm, Feno saw Esebu the blue butterfly.

"I've got news for you," Esebu said. "Koli and his cronies are heading to the hidden spring.

Edi told him about you and the secret water source."

"Oh, no," Negu said. "What shall we do now?"

"Koli may be going to block the way to keep us away from the spring," Feno said.

"Koli hasn't changed. He'll probably be happy to get rid of us this time," Negu said.

"That will be it for us," Feno said.

Esebu just listened.

"Let's wait for your mother. I think we should join Koli's camp," Negu said.

The suggestion to befriend Koli for protection overwhelmed Feno. He dragged himself away from the date palm tree and stood alone for a while. He counted his rather slow heartbeats to quiet the anger that was surging in him like a volcano ready to erupt. After a few minutes, Feno felt as if he was dreaming while wide awake. In the reverie, he had an insight on how to conquer Koli.

Esebu flew to Feno and perched on his broken, still-healing shell. She was so light that Feno didn't notice. Then she hopped and fluttered her wings in his face.

Feno jerked out of his quiet time.

"Please don't disturb me when I'm trying to quiet down."

"I'm sorry, and if you don't need my help, I'll go away."

"Oh, no, don't go away," Feno said. "Actually, you are the one who can help us."

"How?" Esebu asked. "I've never been of help to anyone."

"If you can get the honeybees to sting the elephant, we'll reward them with access to those beautiful flowers hidden in the ravine."

"That's impossible to do."

"Why?"

"The bees have left Tutiland. No rains, no plants. No plants, no flowers. No flowers, no bees."

"It's hopeless," Negu said.

"I haven't lost hope yet," Feno said.

"If there's something else I can do for you, I'll gladly be at your service," Esebu said.

"Maybe some stragglers are still around," Negu said.

"It may take me a while to get to their last colony and back," Esebu said.

"When you find any honeybees left behind, please persuade them to attack Koli," Feno said.

Chapter 16

Esebu found a small swarm of bees that had stayed behind.

"I need your help," Esebu said to the bees.

"What can we do for you?"

"My friends the tortoise family have been bullied by Koli, and they need your help."

"How?"

"Attack Koli."

"You know we hate Koli."

"Of course, I know."

"But we've decided to leave him alone."

"He hasn't left others alone."

"We can't fight others' battles."

"We really need your help."

"What's in it for us?"

"Tortoise Feno knows a secret spring with flowers he wants to reveal to you."

"Flowers with nectar in this drought?"

"Yes."

"Did you want us to attack Koli?"

"Sting him."

"No, we can't do it."

"Why not?"

"When we sting, we die. Try the wasps," Ogba, the honeybee leader, said. "Can you show us where Koli is?"

Esebu directed them. The honeybees set out for the ravine, and Esebu flew back to report to her friends.

Would they ask the wasps instead of the honeybees to help them?

Chapter 17

The elephant, the white crane, the dung beetle, the beaver, the rabbit, and the spider waited at the entrance to the ravine.

"I'm not sure if I want to go down there," the rabbit said.

"You aren't too big to fall into the abyss," Koli said.

"Anything can fall into the ravine," Edi said and hopped off Koli's hump.

The beaver ran to inspect a hole in a dry wood.

Although Koli could not go into the ravine, he could not see why his friends with smaller bodies did not want to seize the opportunity.

"I'm not sure if I want to go down there," the rabbit said.

"Why aren't you eager to go and find the spring?" Koli asked.

"We're afraid," the beaver and the rabbit said together.

"I thought this was a great reward from me to you for your loyalty," Koli said. "It's dangerous down there. But if little tortoise survived it, you, too, can—"

"I hear something crying," the spider interrupted.

They listened for the noise.

"It's a doe," the beaver said, running out of the dry wood.

The rabbit dashed off to find out.

"Get into the ravine," Koli said. "Why bother about the doe?"

"She's in trouble," Edi said.

The beaver came back with a buck.

"My partner, Olulu the doe, has fallen into a pit. She can't get out by herself, and I can't get her out either," the buck said. "Can you help us?"

The buck, lean with hunger, told the story of how Koli saved him some time ago. "Olulu and I were out grazing. I saw shoots of fresh green buds ahead. As I ran for them, I fell into a hole a decaying tree had left behind. Olulu couldn't help me out. I cried for help. After a while, you came to help me. Do you remember?" the buck asked.

"Of course," Koli said. "I'm known for my long memory."

"Can you please save her today?" the buck asked.

"No," Koli said.

All Koli wanted to do was ensure his friends get to the spring before Feno got there.

"No, not now," Koli said.

The buck pleaded. Olulu the doe continued to bell.

"Let's get Olulu out first," Edi said.

"No, maybe later," Koli said.

Just then, Koli raised his trunk. He had an excellent sense of smell. He could sense a whiff of odor three miles away. He raised his head and turned slowly in a full circle to pinpoint the source of the scent. He looked worried.

Chapter 18

Negu and Feno waited for Iage under the date palm.

From a distance they saw a little swarm of honeybees flying in the direction they were heading.

"Did you see the bees that just flew by? Quite unusual to see them at this time," Iage said.

"Yes," Negu said.

"I wonder if Esebu the blue butterfly found them," Feno said.

"What are you talking about?" Iage asked.

"When you lagged behind, Esebu came to let us know that Koli and some of his friends were going to the secret water source," Negu said.

"That was supposed to be our new haven," Iage said.

"Yes," Feno answered.

"I bet Edi told him about it," Iage said.

"You've got that right," Negu said.

"I can't imagine how this would work," Iage said.

"Esebu offered to help us," Negu said.

"And we decided to ask the honeybees to have the job done," Feno said.

"But the bees left the grassland a while ago," Iage said.

"Guess not, since we just saw some fly by," Negu said.

At about the same time, Esebu came to report his conversation with the honeybees. They were unwilling to help.

"The wasps are better than the honeybees," Esebu said.

"Why?" Feno said.

"When honeybees sting, they die," Esebu said.

Negu, Iage, and Feno listened.

"Wasps live to sting another day," Esebu said.

Negu, Iage, and Feno were now close to the ravine's entrance. Koli and his friends were already there. Koli paced around, lifting up his trunk.

Chapter 19

"This is the greatest day in my life," Feno said. "Today, we'll finally overpower Koli."

"You really think so?" Negu asked.

"I can't believe it," Iage said.

"Don't be too sure," Negu said.

"I agree," Iage said.

"Nothing in life is certain," Negu said.

"This looks like a dangerous gamble," Iage said.

"Should we ask the honeybees or the wasps to attack Koli?" Feno asked.

"Let's ask the wasps," Negu said.

"They are too deadly," Iage said.

"Don't we want to do away with Koli?" Negu asked.

"Definitely," Feno said.

"But I've already contacted the honeybees," Esebu said.

"They can't," Feno said.

"They will lose some lives," Iage said.

A swarm of honeybees flew past them.

"We need direction," Ogba, the honeybee leader, said to the blue butterfly.

"The tortoise family still wants you to help them," Esebu said.

"We can't give our lives for them," Ogba said. "Let them get the wasps instead."

"Where can we find them?" Esebu asked.

"They are no more in Tutiland," Ogba said.

"Blue butterfly, you've been so good; please help us to complete what you began," Iage said. "Ask the honeybees to do the job for us. Take them to the entrance leading to the secret water source. In fact, take them to the flowers. As far as I'm concerned their work is done."

"That's crazy," Feno said.

"Are you serious?" Negu asked.

"Totally," Iage replied.

"And the wasps?" Negu asked.

"They have left Tutiland," Feno said.

"Why would you pay for a task that hasn't yet been done?" Feno asked.

"I want to instill fear into Koli rather than kill him," Iage said.

"Honeybees will do a better job than wasps. What do you imagine would happen if the wasps attacked Koli?"

"The wasps would swarm around Koli," Feno said.

"Some would fly into his hollow trunk," Negu said.

"And sting its soft inner lining," Feno said.

"Yes," Negu said.

"Others would attack his eyes," Feno said.

"And we'd look on with satisfaction as he struggles," Iage said.

"Running around like a frightened bull," Feno said.

"In a zigzag," Negu said.

"Falling down," Feno said.

"And rising up again," Negu said.

"The wasps pursuing and stinging him," Feno said.

"Overpowered, he'd fall one last time," Negu said.

"And that would be the end of it," Feno said.

"That *won't* be the end of it," Iage said. "His friends—those who trusted him—would be there: the white crane, the dung beetle, and all the others. They will still be there," Iage said.

"But we would be free," Feno said. "There would be no one that big and strong in their camp to terrorize us anymore."

"What's the point when we're free at the expense of others?" Iage asked.

"We were the underdogs until now," Negu said.

"That's how he treated us," Feno said.

"Why should we just replace him, turn around, and do what we hated when it was done to us?"

"What do you mean?" Negu asked.

"Why should we destroy him when we didn't want to be destroyed?" Iage answered with a question.

"Because when he gets the chance, he will kill us first," Negu said. "The honeybees are on our side. We can do whatever we want now."

Chapter 20

Iage was surprised at Negu's suggestion that they could do anything they wanted since the honeybees were now in their camp.

"It's true the honeybees are on our side. But we *can't* do anything we want," Iage said.

There was a long silence.

"What's the point of having power if we can't use it?" Negu asked.

"We can use power in many ways," Iage said.

"How?" Negu asked.

"By remembering what it was like when we were the underdogs," Iage said.

"You're so naïve," Negu said.

"Naïve or not, here's what I propose. Elephants are known to have great memories. Koli won't forget if we scare him enough. That way we won't have his blood on our hands. We can get him to do all that's right for all of us. Not just for his friends but for all of us. That, in my opinion, is the best way to use our power—the only way to bring peace and the only way for us to be truly free."

"If you want to instill fear in Koli, honeybees flying by him alone won't get the work done," Feno said.

"I agree," Negu said and nodded.

"Let's devise a way to have the bees harass him without actually stinging him," Feno said. "Then no bees would have to die."

"Let's tell him what we really want him to do as our leader," Negu suggested.

"And let's give him a piece of our minds," Feno said.

The tortoise family decided to rely on the honeybees instead of the wasps. Esebu the blue butterfly led the bees to the entrance to the ravine where Koli was standing. The buck and the others were pleading for stranded Olulu.

The bees flew past Koli's large ears. He

flapped them so vigorously that it appeared they would fall off his head. The bees perched and crawled on his trunk without stinging him. Koli jumped around, raised his front legs and trunk, and brought them down again.

Just then a latecomer bee, unaware of the new plan, stung Koli in his left eye.

Trumpeting thundering sounds for help, Koli ran loose in the open grassland, falling down, rising up, running in circles, and returning to the entrance of the ravine where he fell and could not rise.

Still, the other honeybees buzzed around him without a sting. His friends looked on, scared, confused, and helpless. Soon a loose circle of onlookers formed around the elephant king.

Negu, Iage, and Feno joined the onlookers. Their unconquerable enemy could not rise from his fall because of the honeybees' relentless harassment.

From high up in the sky, Nakutu the eagle witnessed what was happening. She informed the mother lion and the other animals Koli had terrorized the previous evening. Nakutu was

Trumpeting thundering sounds for help, Koli ran loose in the open grassland.

surprised that Tsali the lion hadn't died in the fight with Koli. He had survived it and gone home to his wife and young cubs.

Tsali, still weakened, came limping with his wife and little ones to witness the once-in-a-lifetime event.

Tutilanders looked on in surprise as Koli fell on his left side and shook his head with one swollen eye. Because he'd exhausted himself, it was a struggle for him to rise from the ground. He flapped his large ears. He pulled his weight and dragged himself up. He fell down. The honeybees buzzed louder and swarmed faster about him. They crawled around his eyes, ears, and trunk. A few of the onlookers ran away because they feared Koli was going to attack. The constant harassment dragged on.

Chapter 21

Koli fell back on the ground each time he attempted to rise up.

"Stop now. Enough," Negu said to the honeybees. "Stop, but don't leave yet. There's something more."

The honeybees could not hear him. They continued the harassment. Negu finally asked Esebu to implore the bees to stop.

Koli felt relieved. He was surprised to see that it was Negu who was saving him.

Negu, Iage, and Feno approached a subdued Koli.

"Thank you for sparing my life. For making the terrible honeybees go away," Koli said, gasping for breath.

"You're welcome," Negu, Iage, and Feno said in one voice.

"What can I do to repay you?" Koli asked.

"What we've always wanted you to do for us," Iage said.

"Be our fair, just, and caring ruler," Negu said.

"Nature blessed you with immense power. Use it to help all of us, especially the weak among us," Feno said.

"Yes, I will," Koli said. "I'm so sorry for letting you, my subjects, down. I had forgotten how terrible it feels to be helpless."

"Honestly, we don't hate you for being powerful. You pushed us away from you because you were selfish, brutal, and ruthless in bringing death to others. You could easily have won our friendship with your kindness," Negu said.

Tsali, the convalescing lion, limped to the middle of the circle. Tutilanders clapped for him.

"Thank you, thank you," Tsali said. The applause drowned his voice. He paused for the shouting and clapping to die down.

"I'll be brief. Welcome back, Feno," Tsali

said. "We all thought the ravine swallowed you up. I'm so glad to see you." He paused. "Negu, I find it difficult to understand you and your family. You're forgiving this tyrant who almost took your life and mine. You're forgiving this monster who nearly killed your son. In fact, your daughter died because he denied you water. I'm confused. Sorry, but I can't reconcile with Koli. And I'd like tortoise Feno to be our new king."

"Yes. Let's make Feno our new king," some of the Tutilanders shouted.

"He is young," the spider shouted.

"Energetic," Atini the giraffe yelled.

"Intelligent," Nakutu the eagle said.

"Fearless," Roko the monkey said.

"Thank you," Feno said.

The shouts of joy and clapping went on. After they died down, Fear-No-One cleared his throat and said, "I'm really honored." Then he called his parents aside.

"What a brilliant idea," Iage whispered.

"You'll make a great leader," Negu said, suppressing his excitement.

"I'm not sure about that," Feno said.

"You know what it is to suffer," Iage said.

"What has suffering to do with being a leader?" Feno said.

"Everything, my son," Negu said.

"Caring, my baby," Iage said.

"Suffering breeds caring, and caring is the soul of leadership," Negu said.

"Feno, don't you have anything to say—" Iage said but was interrupted.

"We've lost a bee," Esebu announced.

"Oh, no, that's terrible," Iage said.

"Let's inform Tutilanders, so we all can mourn him," Feno said.

Chapter 22

When Feno came back to the gathering, everyone was cheering. They were expecting his acceptance speech.

"I have sad news for you," Feno said. "One of our fighters, honeybee Arrow, has died."

Noises of sorrow seized the crowd. Disbelief, sadness, and then gratitude to Arrow for helping to subdue Koli.

"Arrow is our hero," someone shouted.

"Let's observe a minute of silence in honor of our fallen hero," Feno said.

"Hail, our new king," Roko the monkey

interrupted before the one-minute silence was over.

"Yes, Feno is our man," Tsali said.

The crowd began to clap and shout, "Feno is our new king."

After a while, the young tortoise, who had just turned twenty-three—which is roughly equivalent to twelve years for a human being—motioned to calm them down.

"Thank you, brave lion," Feno said. "Thank you, Roko. Yes. Everyone thought I was dead. I was thrown into the ravine to die, but I survived. Thank you all for wanting me to be your leader. Before I say anything at all about whether I can accept your offer, let me thank all those who helped me.

"I thank my father and mother for willing to risk their lives for me. When they thought I was dead, they were ready to do all it took so that my death would mean something.

"Next, I want to thank Esebu the blue butterfly. You've been my friend for many years. You helped us to contact the honeybees. Just so you know: the honeybees are here to stay."

Huge applause interrupted the speech.

"They've agreed to stay around. We owe the bees a great deal. Our gratitude goes especially to honeybee Arrow, who gave his life for the cause. This victory isn't the victory of one individual or one family. It's a victory for the entire Tutiland community.

"I thank Tsali from the bottom of my heart for standing up to Koli." Feno turned to Tsali. "You risked your life and fought for what you believed in. Thank you for coming here when you're in so much pain. And thank you for proposing that I be the next king."

"It's a pleasure," Tsali said and bowed. "But I still think Koli deserves to be punished."

"Much as I would like to be king," Feno continued, "I honestly feel that Koli should remain king of the grassland."

"No, we want you," Roko yelled.

The shrieking and yelling of the gathering drowned Feno's words. He paused to allow the crowd to quiet down.

"Koli has been humiliated enough. That's his punishment. Moreover, he has already given us his word. He is a strong and unifying figure. There's nothing to fear since we now have the necessary checks and balances in place. We'll offer him the opportunity to show his gratitude. He'll do this by serving as the wonderful leader he was meant to be."

Feno saw a herd of elephants approaching from the horizon. Relatives who had deserted Koli several years earlier galloped up to join the Tutilanders.

Chapter 23

The returning elephants formed a circle around Koli, who still lay exhausted and subdued on the ground. They took turns locking their trunks with his.

"From far away, we heard your cry for help," Efoye, the matriarch elephant, said. "We noticed something in you had changed. You weren't afraid to cry for help. You acknowledged that you were vulnerable."

Feno mounted a small hill so he could be visible to the gathering.

"Welcome, elephants. Today is a great day for all of us," Feno said.

"My parents and I know that as members of

the tortoise clan, we'll live at least for a hundred and fifty years before we die. We'll outlive you all, even the giant lizard. The best we can do is to allow Koli to remain king. We'll be guardians of Tutiland's memory. That way we'll be there to settle any problems that may come up during any future crisis. I shall not be king."

There was dead silence. Efoye, the matriarch elephant, dragged herself closer to Feno. "We're here to support Koli if you still trust him," she said. "We've come to help him be a caring ruler."

Negu, Iage, and Feno went to Koli and together attempted to help him rise up.

Koli wiped his bee-stung left eye with his fan-shaped ear. He motioned to them that he had something to say.

"I'm sorry to have offended you. Sorry for being cruel to you all." Koli struggled to rise up on his own but could not. "My cruelties came out of fear for my enemies. It's painful to be brought down by a tiny honeybee, and it made me feel so helpless."

Silence covered the gathering like a healing mist.

"We understand and forgive you," the homecoming elephants said.

"Look what being afraid of his enemies has done to the most powerful one in Tutiland!" Feno said.

Chapter 24

Koli raised his front right leg to show he was ready to be lifted up. Negu, Iage, and Feno drew closer. Together with all the visiting elephants, they assisted the fallen king to his feet. Onlookers cheered, laughed, and cried.

Negu then asked to speak. "We can't force our child to be king if he doesn't want to." He paused and moved away from the circle they formed around Koli.

"We love to be in your company," Efoye, the matriarch elephant, said.

The lizard said, "I remember Koli when he was caring, strong, and trustworthy."

"That was the past. He's now a tyrant," the lion interrupted, as he limped forward to attack

Koli. "He must be punished."

"No more fighting," Iage shouted.

Lion staggered back.

"We're starting a new era today," Feno said.

"You're going to let him get away with everything?" Tsali asked.

"Let's ask him what he plans to do," Iage said.

"I feel weak now," Koli stuttered. "But someone struggling in a pit somewhere needs my help this moment. I should have rescued her earlier. I can start with her."

"Who's that?" Feno asked.

"Olulu," the buck and Edi shouted in unison.

"Let's do it," Efoye said.

Buck led them to Olulu, who was lying helpless and half asleep in the pit. She had exhausted herself after struggling to jump out for several hours without success.

King Koli was out of breath, too. Efoye pushed him aside. Koli bounced back. "Let me do it," he said.

"You're so weak," the matriarch said.

They all watched as he pulled Olulu out with his trunk.

"I can," Koli said.

They all watched as he pulled Olulu out with his trunk.

The onlookers cheered. Olulu looked surprised at the crowd that had come to her rescue.

"It feels good to be part of a caring community," Olulu said.

Koli continued his speech. "I want to make up for the past. With the help of the matriarch and all the elephants, we'll rebuild the bridge."

The crowd applauded.

"That's not enough. I want all of us to have access to the lake," Lion said.

"But it's drying out," Zagadu the dung beetle said.

"There isn't enough for all of us," Edi said.

"Let's ration it then," Roko the monkey said.

"Let's pause and see if we can come up with another solution," Feno said.

"There's no other solution," Roko said.

"Oh, I know...the spring," Esebu the blue butterfly said.

"We can't get to it," Atini the giraffe yelled.

Chapter 25

After discussing these options, they came up with a plan. The birds and butterflies explored the dangerous hillside and found two additional springs. The burrowing animals were able to dig a trench through which the spring emptied into a pond accessible to all of them.

Koli, Efoye, and the rest of the elephants rebuilt the bridge. They also built two new ones. Tutilanders could travel to the forest for food and back to their drought-stricken grassland home. Although the drought worsened, Tutilanders were happier because of the newfound bond the crisis had forged in them.

Several months after these events happened, one afternoon, the sky turned dark, frightening the cubs, the nestlings, and other little creatures playing outside. Those who could do so ran as fast as possible to their parents. At first, the parents could not figure out what the problem was.

"Look up," a cub said to his mother. "Darkness is covering the sky at midday."

Many of the young ones had never seen rain clouds form. For them, it was an unusual happening.

"These are rain-bearing clouds," the lioness said.

Thunder rolled. Lightning struck. The little creatures had never seen anything like it before. The heavy rains that began that afternoon lasted for three days. When the rains stopped, the dry riverbanks overflowed. The streams and pond the community had built were washed away.

Plants began to grow. The dead trees came back to life. Mushrooms grew once more on the hillside. There was now enough for everyone.

Koli gathered Tutilanders for a celebration.

"We're ending the water rationing in place these past several months," Koli told his people.

Tortoise Feno's dream of a land flowing with rivers and flourishing plants had come to pass

"We've survived the drought. We shall be thirsty no more. Let's celebrate."

Koli kept his word. He remained king for many years until his death.

One by one, the Tutiland generation who experienced the Great Drought all died except the tortoise clan, who remained in their ancestral cave.

Tortoise Feno's dream of a land flowing with rivers and flourishing plants had come to pass.

Negu and Iage had more children. Their children had their own.

Feno became a father, then a grandfather, and then a great-grandfather.

Because they lived long, the tortoise family became keepers of the secret of surviving a drought.

Epilogue

Now you have the secret of surviving a drought.

About the Author

Author Kwami Nyamidie is an award-winning poet who grew up in Togo, West Africa, before migrating with his family to Ghana after they left their cocoa farms amid civil unrest. Nyamidie holds an MA in transforming spirituality from Seattle University and a specialization certificate in creative writing from Wesleyan University. Now a US citizen, Nyamidie lives in the Pacific Northwest and works with a library.

About the Illustrator

Nicole Stremlow Monahan was born and raised in the midwest were she spent hours upon hours looking at children's books in her mother's bookstore. After graduating from the University of Illinois, Monahan worked as an architect and art director. Today, she is an illustrator and art instructor working out of her studio and across the world. Monahan loves spending time with her family in the Pacific Northwest.

Made in the USA
San Bernardino, CA
03 April 2017